RED and

BLUE

GREEN and WHITE

Inspired by a true story

Words by
LEE WIND

pictures by
PAUL O. ZELINSKY

LQ
LEVINE QUERIDO

MONTCLAIR | AMSTERDAM | HOBOKEN

Across the street, Isaac lit his
family's decorative menorah,
and his house glowed
Blue and White.

Later, when it was dark and everyone was asleep, shadows approached Isaac's house.

SMASH!

The window shattered.
A stone!
Shards of glass falling.

And Isaac, wide awake, watched their menorah flicker out.

The adults talked, and talked.
"You'll sleep in our room for now,"
his dad told Isaac and his sister.

Isaac's mom asked, "Should we light the menorah again?"

If they didn't, Isaac knew it would be like hiding they were Jewish.

That didn't feel right.

The next night, Isaac lit the menorah, and
through the new window, his house glowed.

Across the street, Teresa watched the menorah come on, and let out a breath she hadn't known she was holding.

She took out paper, and markers, and drew.

When she was done, Teresa added two
words, and put the drawing up in the window.
Through the paper, the light shone
Blue and White.

Isaac saw the drawing, and ran outside.

The idea grew...
with more drawings.
Their friends joined in.

Then their school. And their library.

Local stores joined in.
And restaurants.
And clubs.

It was on TV,
and in the newspaper.

Three weeks after Isaac and his family stood tall, and Teresa and her family stood up by their side, their whole town was dressed up to celebrate the true spirit of the holidays — the true meaning of community.

From more than 10,000 windows came

Christmas tree and Menorah
RED AND GREEN AND

BLUE AND WHITE

stronger together

Shining bright

light

Christmas Tree
and Menorah Light
Red and
Green and
Blue and
White

Stronger together
Shining bright

AUTHOR'S NOTE

This book was inspired by the real events of December 1993 in Billings, Montana. Teresa and Isaac are real people too, though I have fictionalized their interactions and some details of how things unfolded. What I hope shines through is how the people in Billings chose to not just stand by and be *BYstanders* while bad things happened to others. Instead, they stood *up* to say the bad things weren't okay. They chose to be *UPstanders*. And when the whole community stood up together for friendship, and respecting differences, and love — the stone-throwers backed down. And in Billings, Montana, love won.

To learn more about the story behind *Red and Green and Blue and White*, check out www.leewind.org.

For Gavi. Use all the colors — that's what they're for. — LW

For Norman. — POZ

This is an Arthur A. Levine book
Published by Levine Querido

LEVINE QUERIDO
www.levinequerido.com
info@levinequerido.com

Levine Querido is distributed by Chronicle Books LLC

Text copyright © 2021 by Lee Wind
Illustrations copyright © 2021 by Paul O. Zelinsky

Library of Congress Control Number: 2020950650
ISBN 978-1-64614-087-9

Printed and bound in China

FSC
www.fsc.org
MIX
Paper from
responsible sources
FSC™ C104723

Published in 2021
First Printing

The illustrations for this book were drawn on a Wacom tablet, in images of up to 150 layers, using brushes of the artist's own creation.

Book design by Charles Kreloff
Text type set in Literata